BLAST TO THE PAST

BY SCOTT NICKEL

ILLUSTRATED BY STEVE HARPSTER

STONE ARCH BOOKS
MINNEAPOLIS   SAN DIEGO

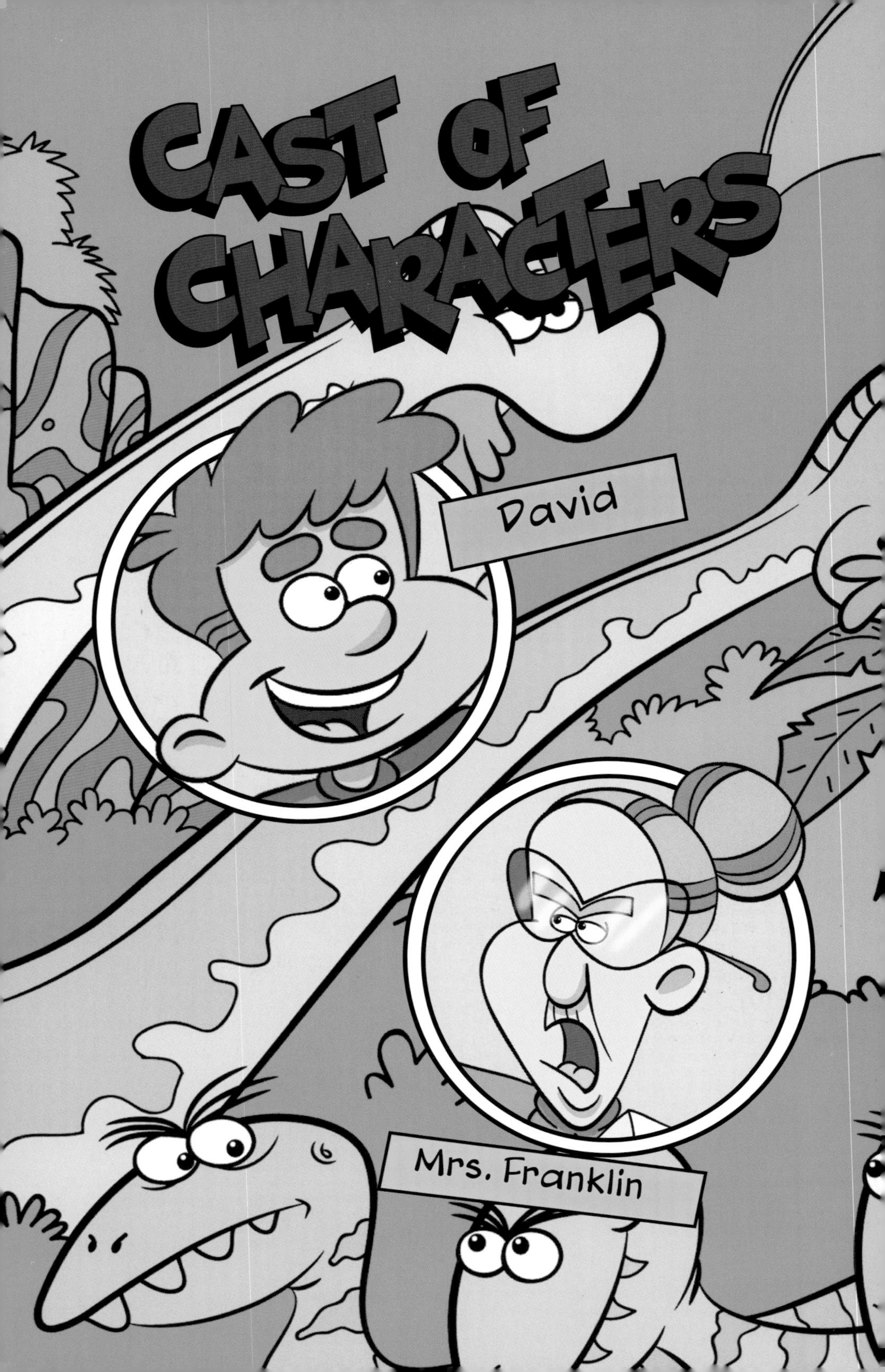
CAST OF CHARACTERS
David
Mrs. Franklin

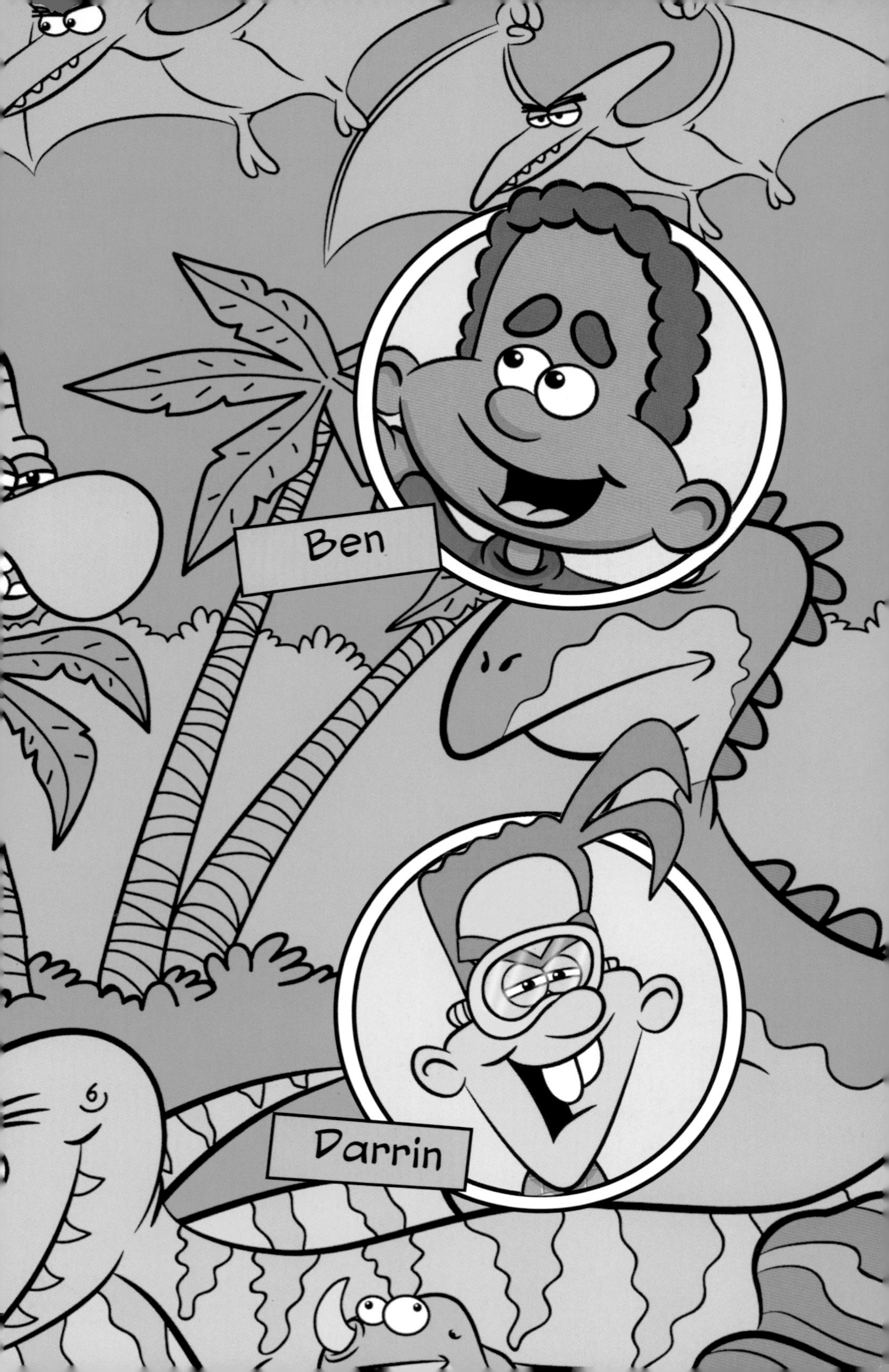
Ben
Darrin

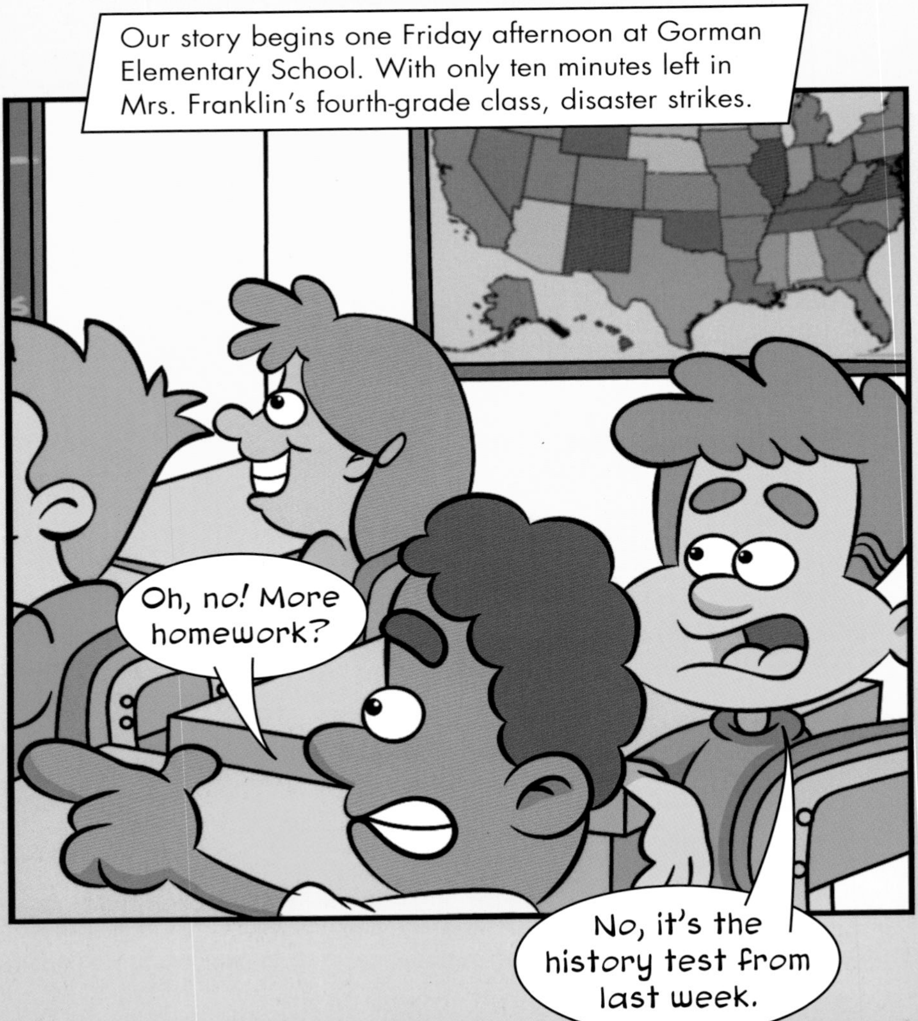
Our story begins one Friday afternoon at Gorman Elementary School. With only ten minutes left in Mrs. Franklin's fourth-grade class, disaster strikes.
Oh, no! More homework?
No, it's the history test from last week.

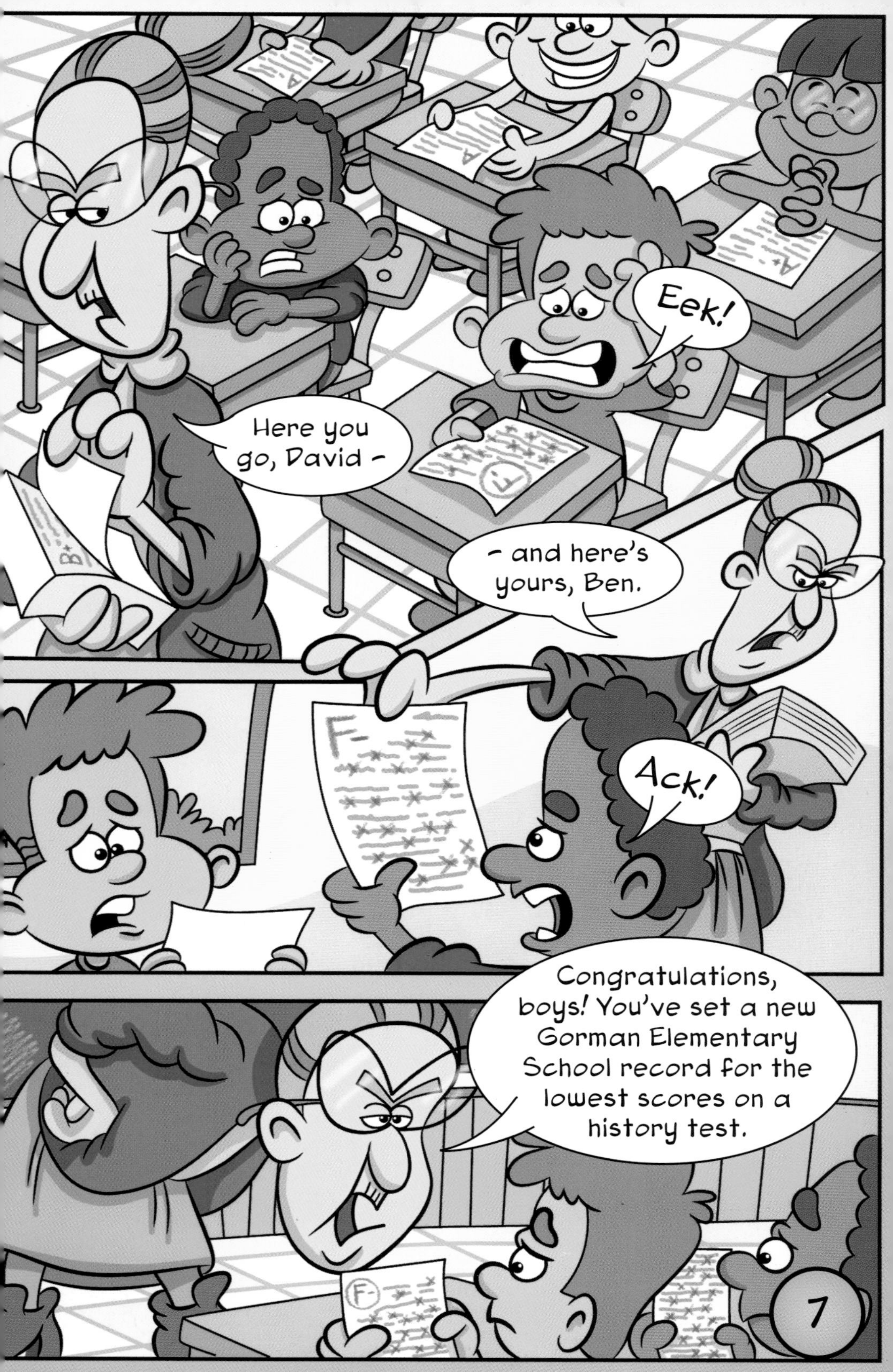
Eek!
Here you go, David -
- and here's yours, Ben.
Ack!
Congratulations, boys! You've set a new Gorman Elementary School record for the lowest scores on a history test.

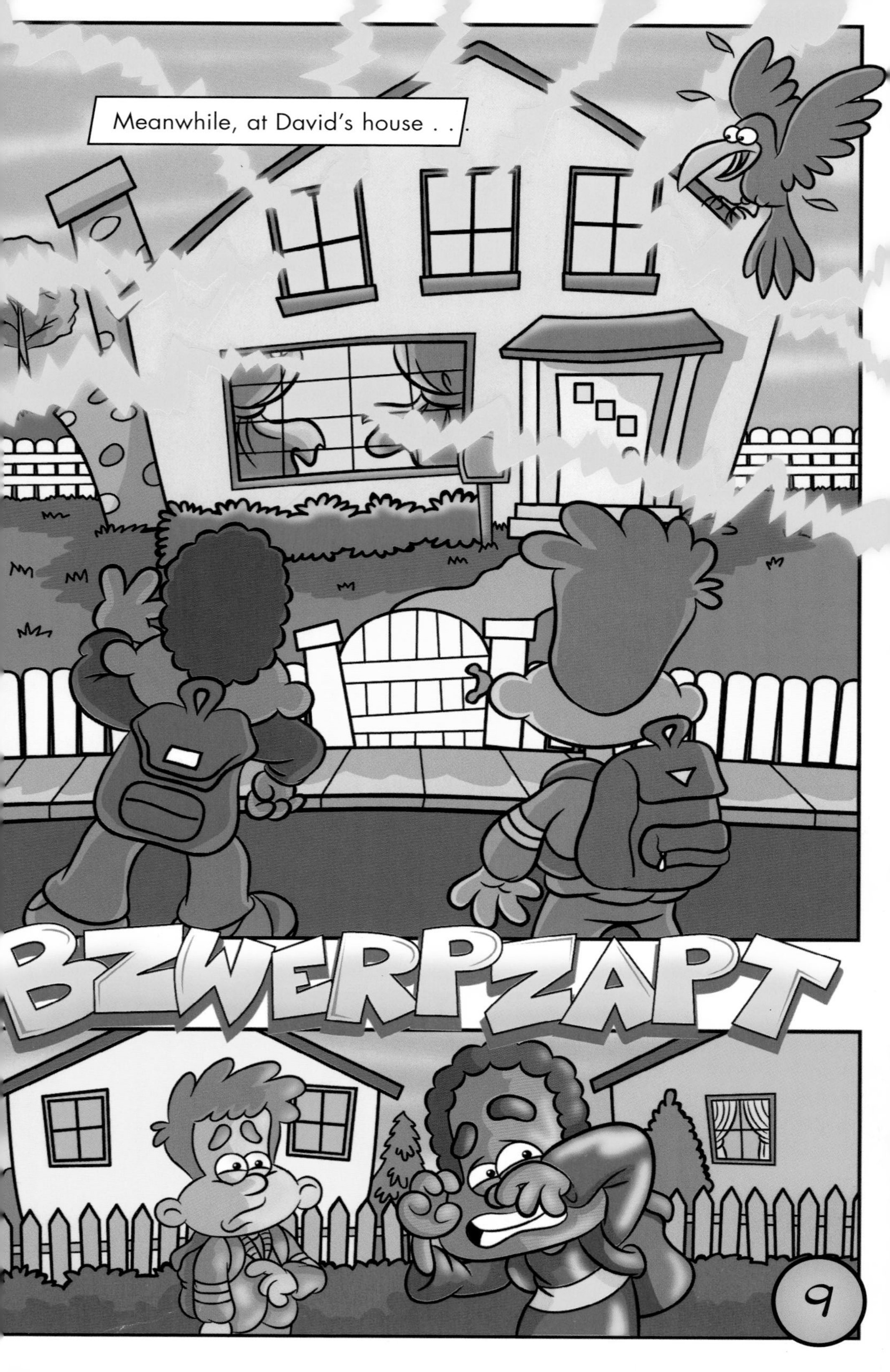
Meanwhile, at David's house . . .
BZWERPZAPT

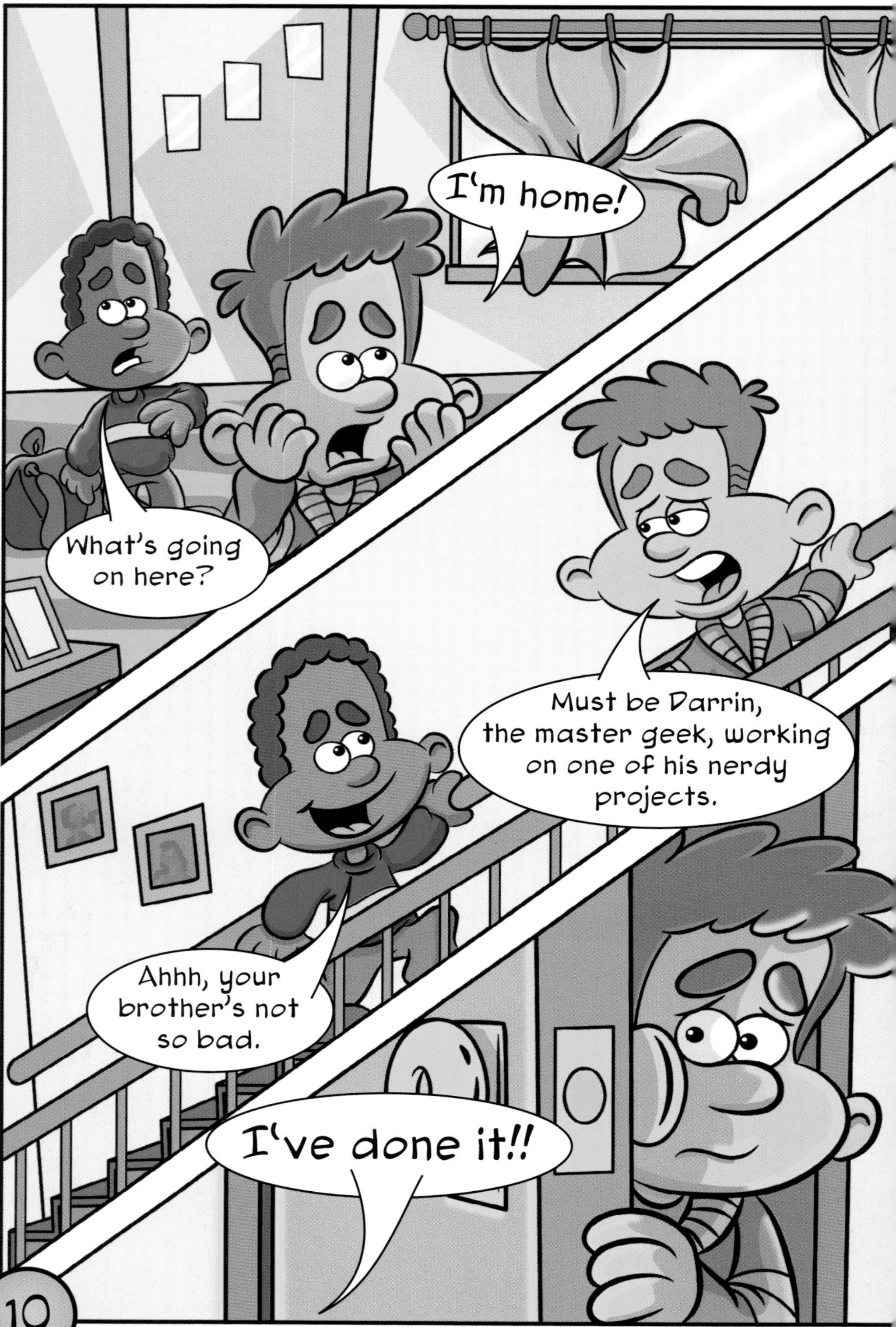
I'm home!
What's going on here?
Must be Darrin, the master geek, working on one of his nerdy projects.
Ahhh, your brother's not so bad.
I've done it!!

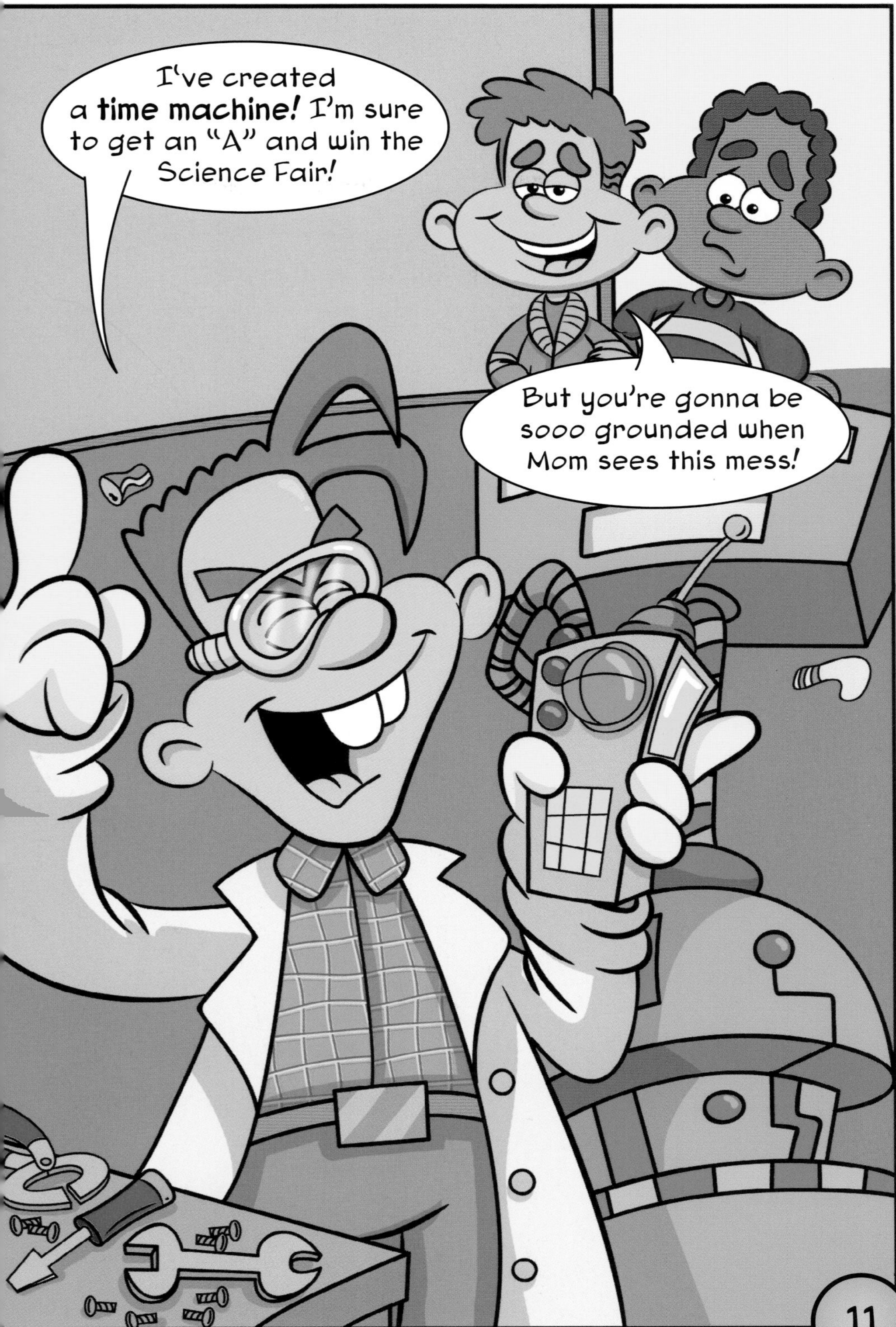
I've created a **time machine!** I'm sure to get an "A" and win the Science Fair!
But you're gonna be sooo grounded when Mom sees this mess!

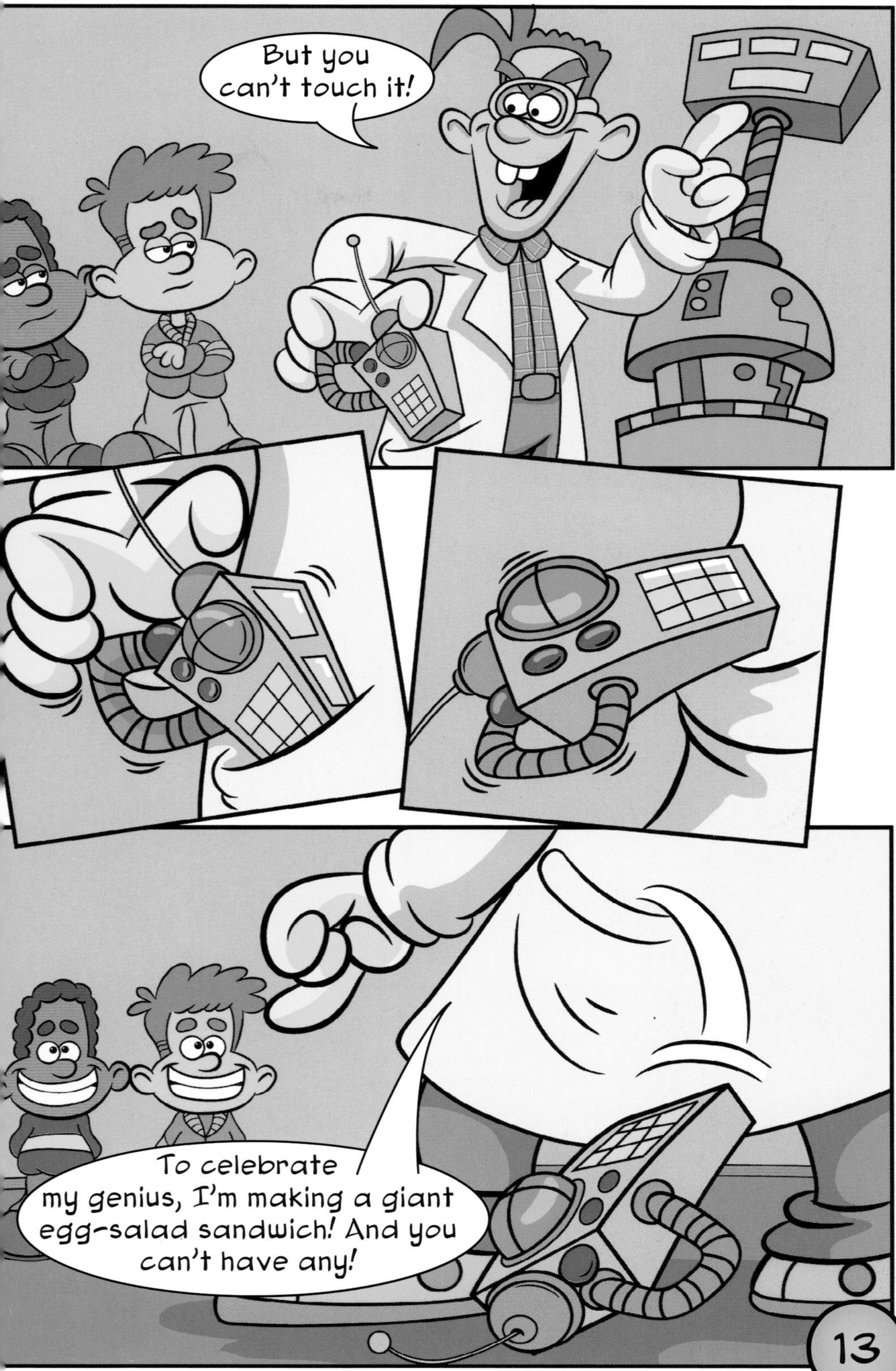
But you can't touch it!
To celebrate my genius, I'm making a giant egg-salad sandwich! And you can't have any!

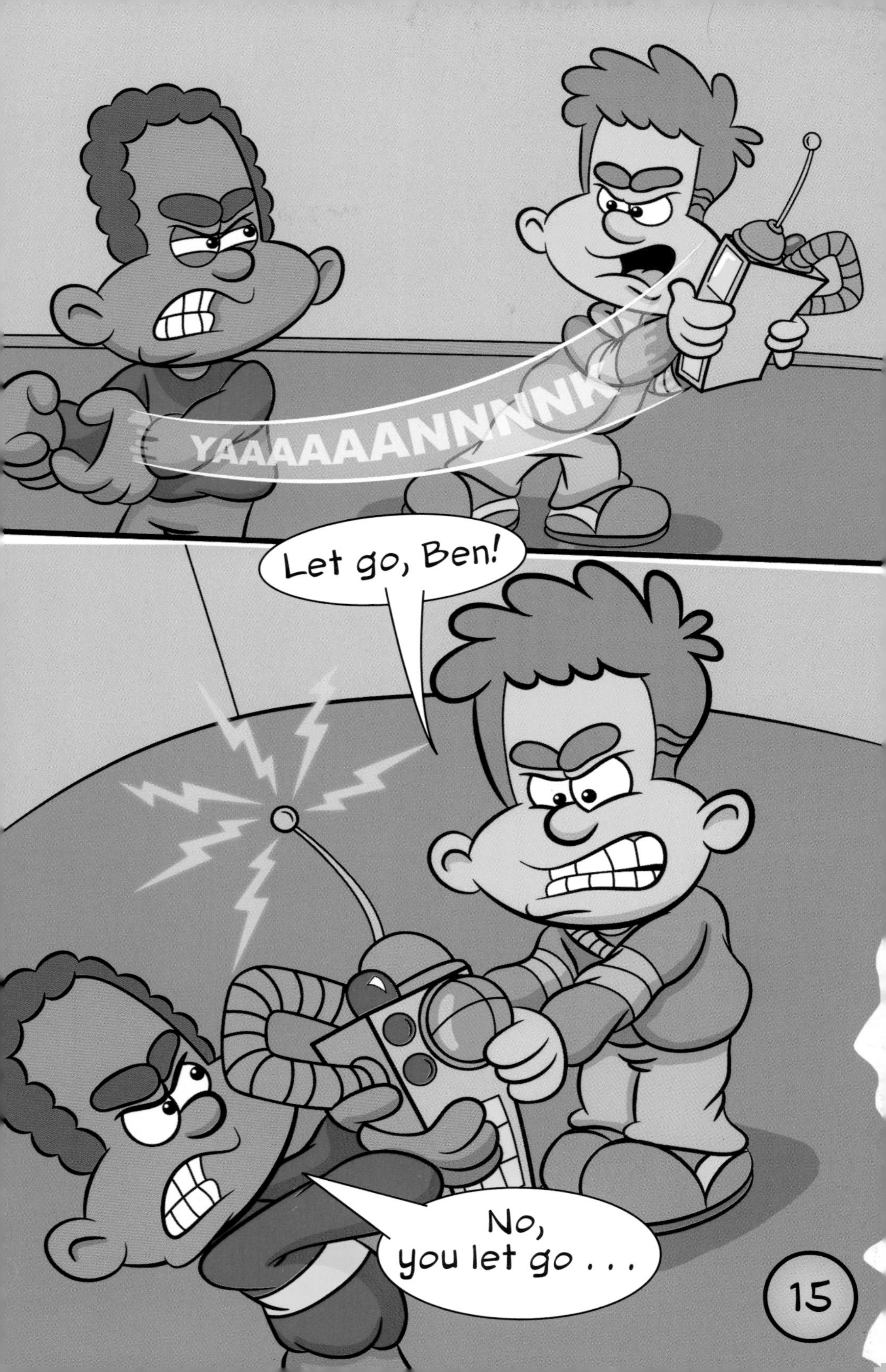
YAAAAAANNNNNK
Let go, Ben!
No, you let go . . .

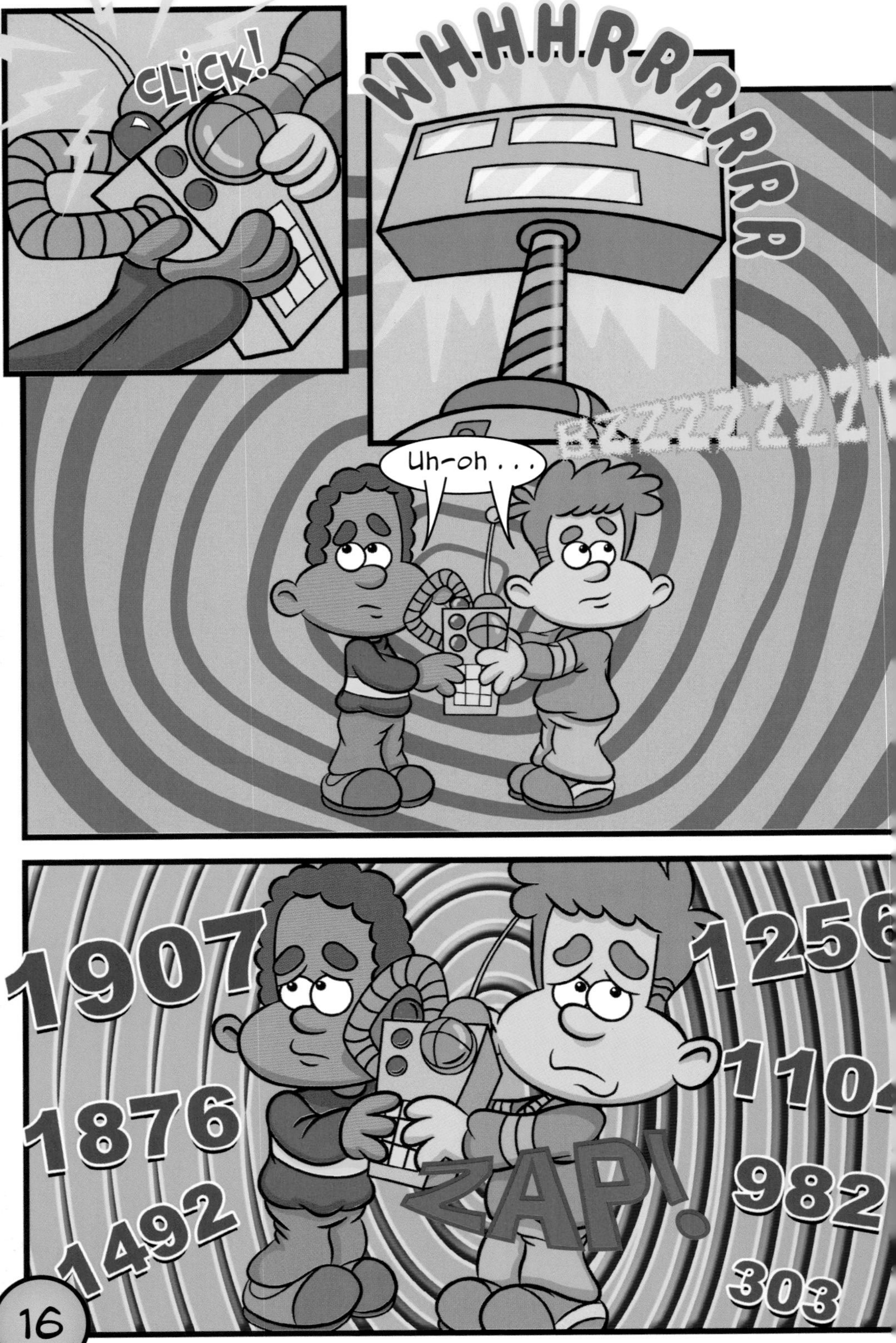
CLICK!
WHHHRRRRRRR
BZZZZZZZZT
Uh-oh . . .
1907
1256
1876
1102
1492
ZAP!
982
303

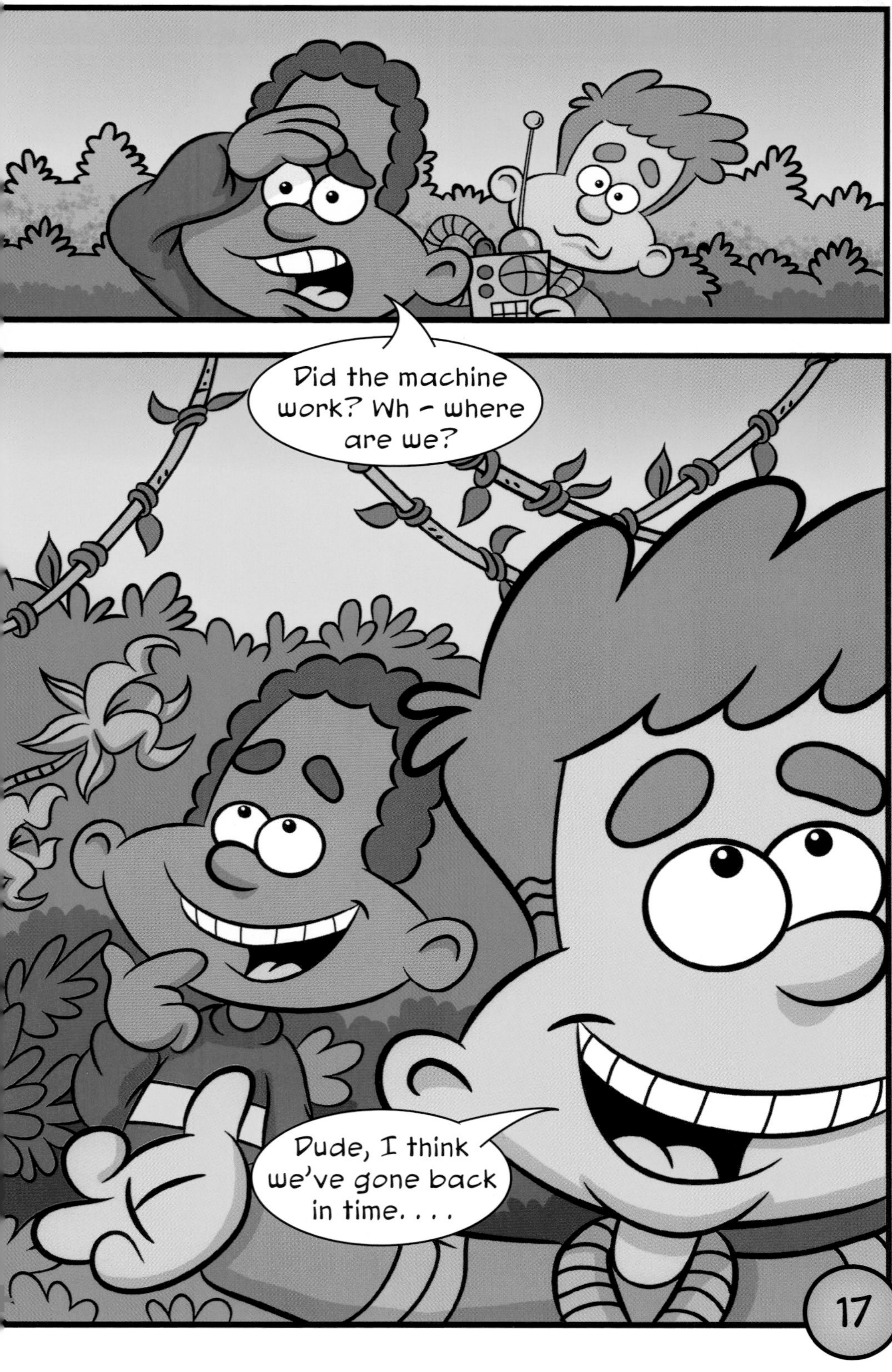
Did the machine work? Wh - where are we?
Dude, I think we've gone back in time. . . .

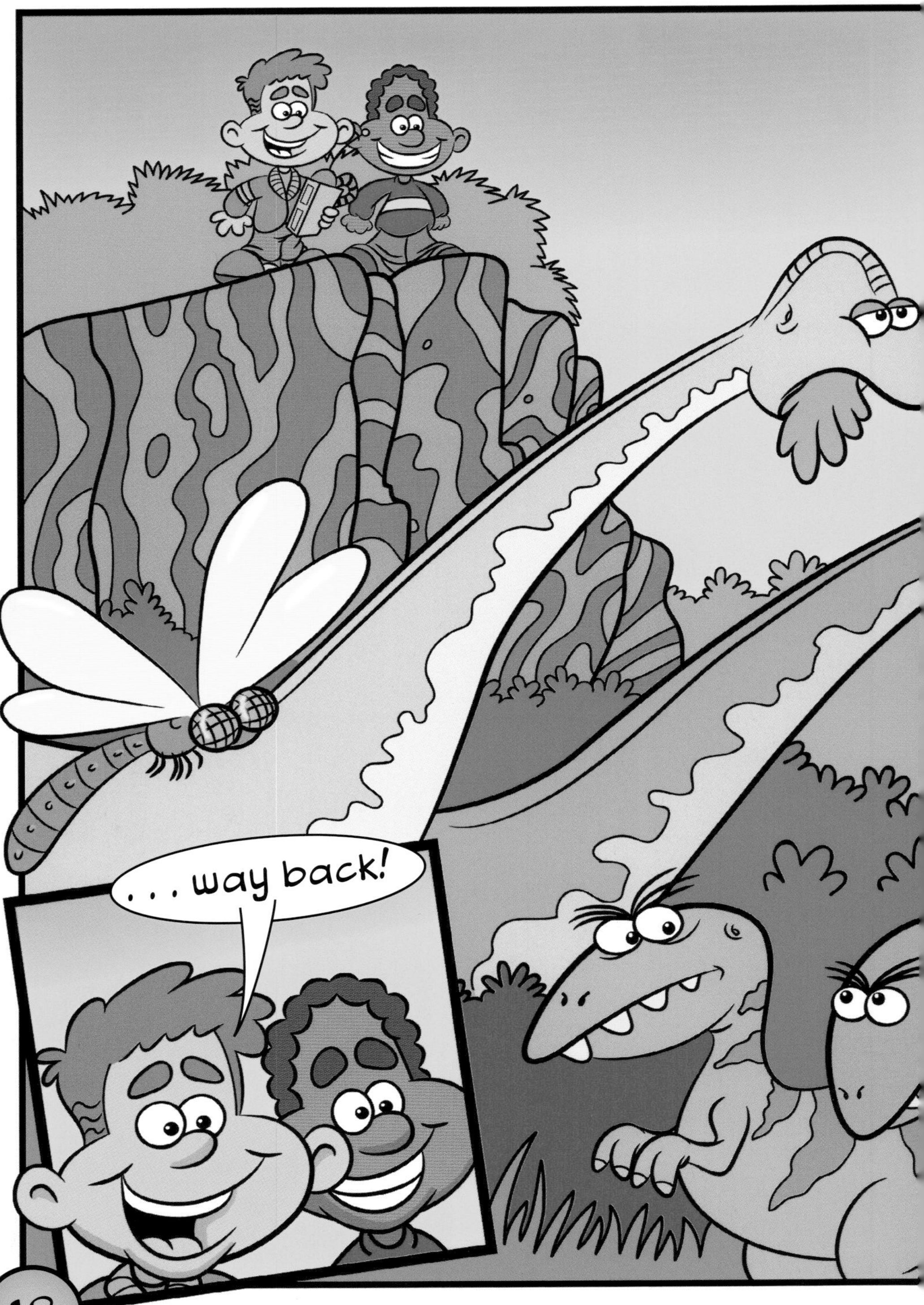
. . . way back!

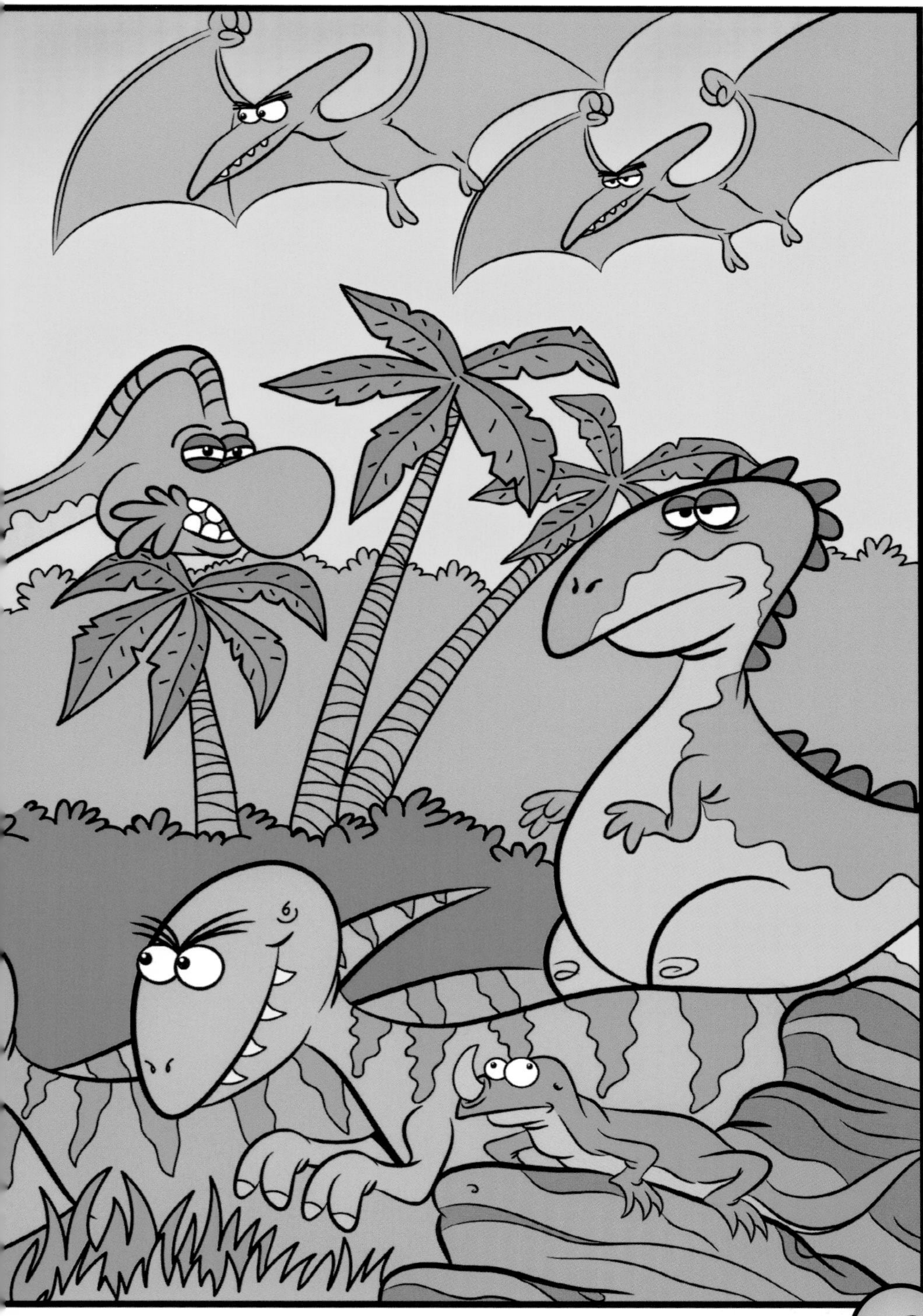

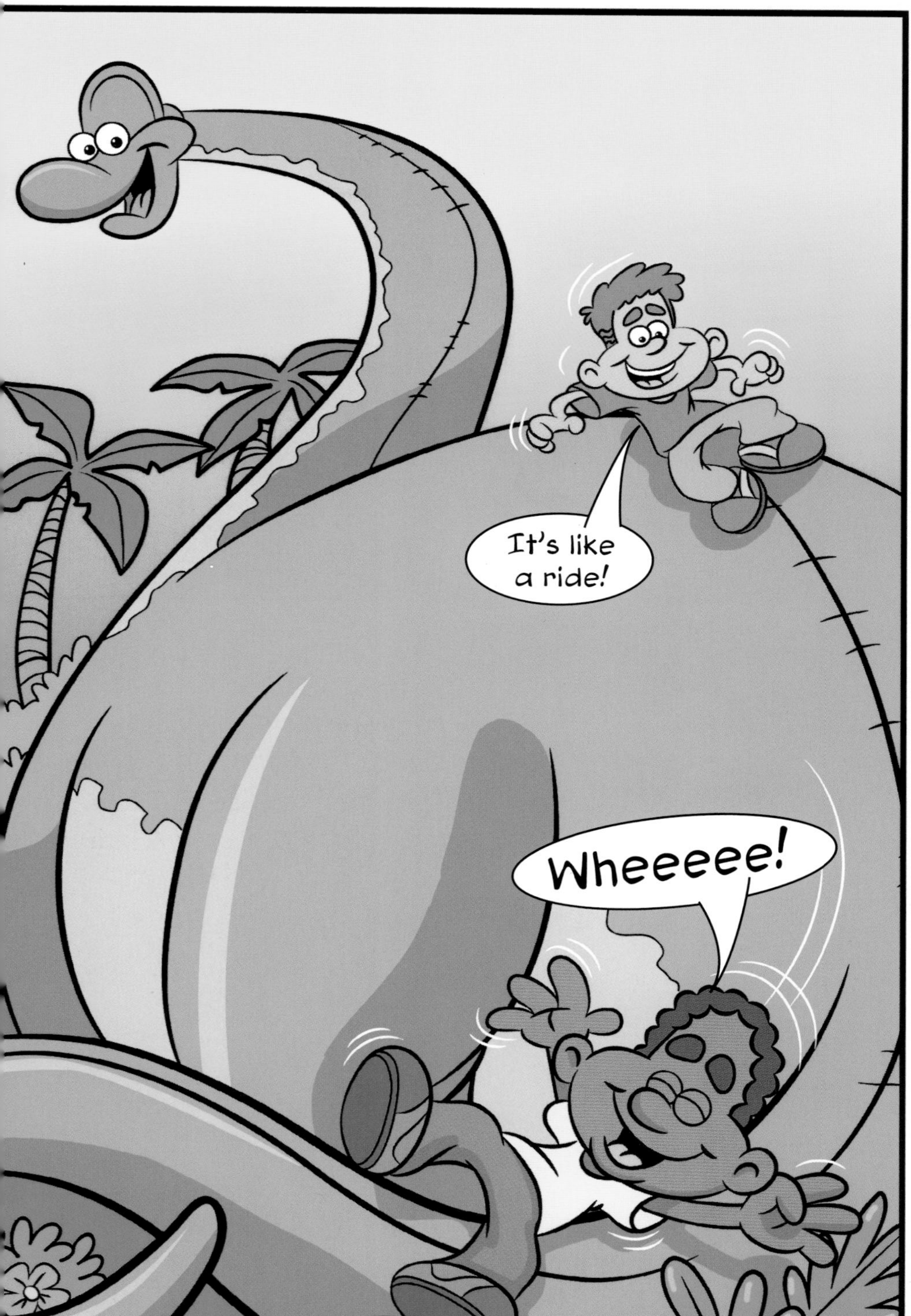
It's like a ride!
Wheeeee!

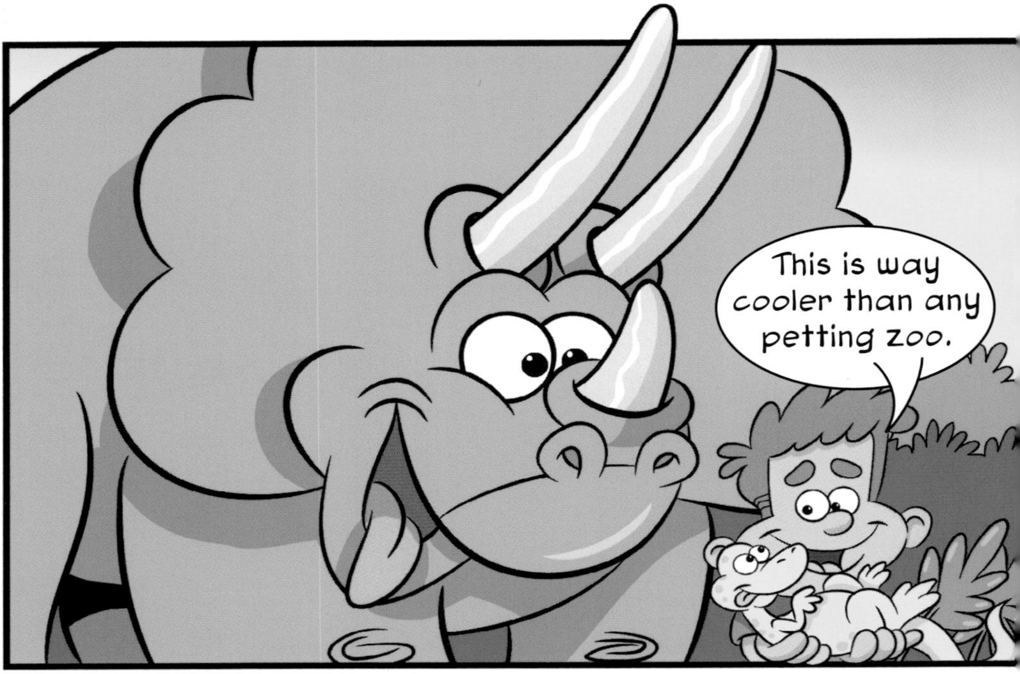
This is way cooler than any petting zoo.

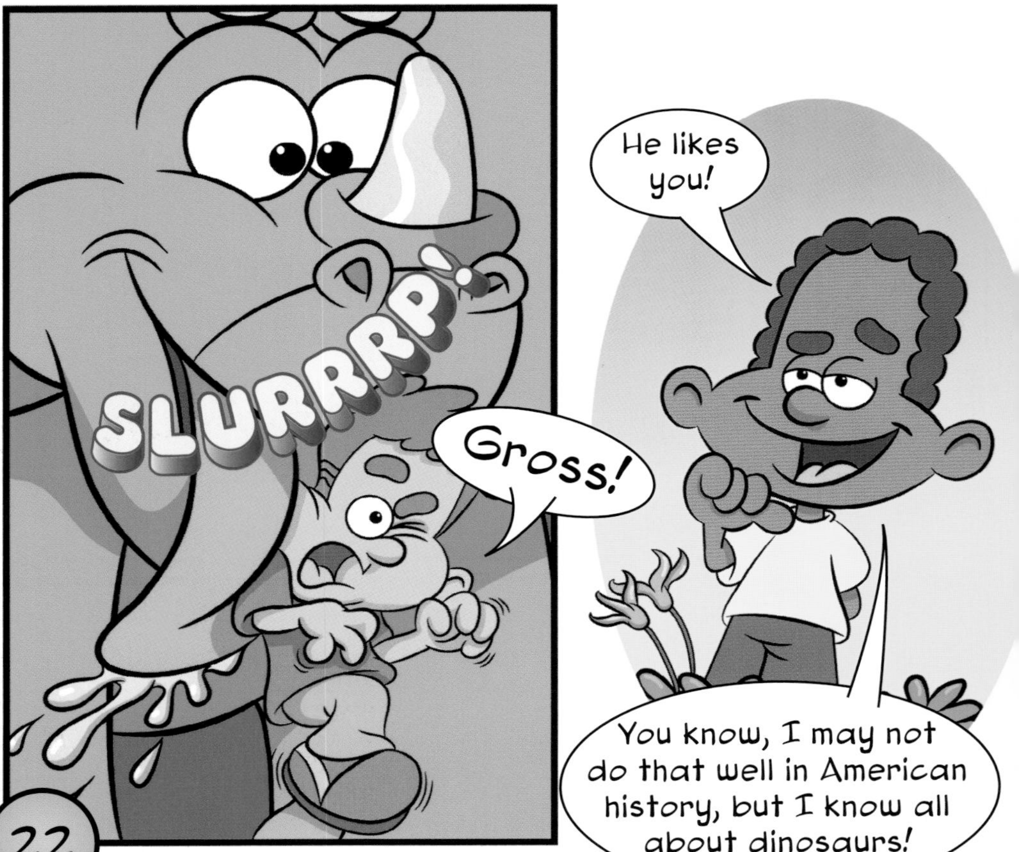
He likes you!
SLURRRP!
Gross!
You know, I may not do that well in American history, but I know all about dinosaurs!

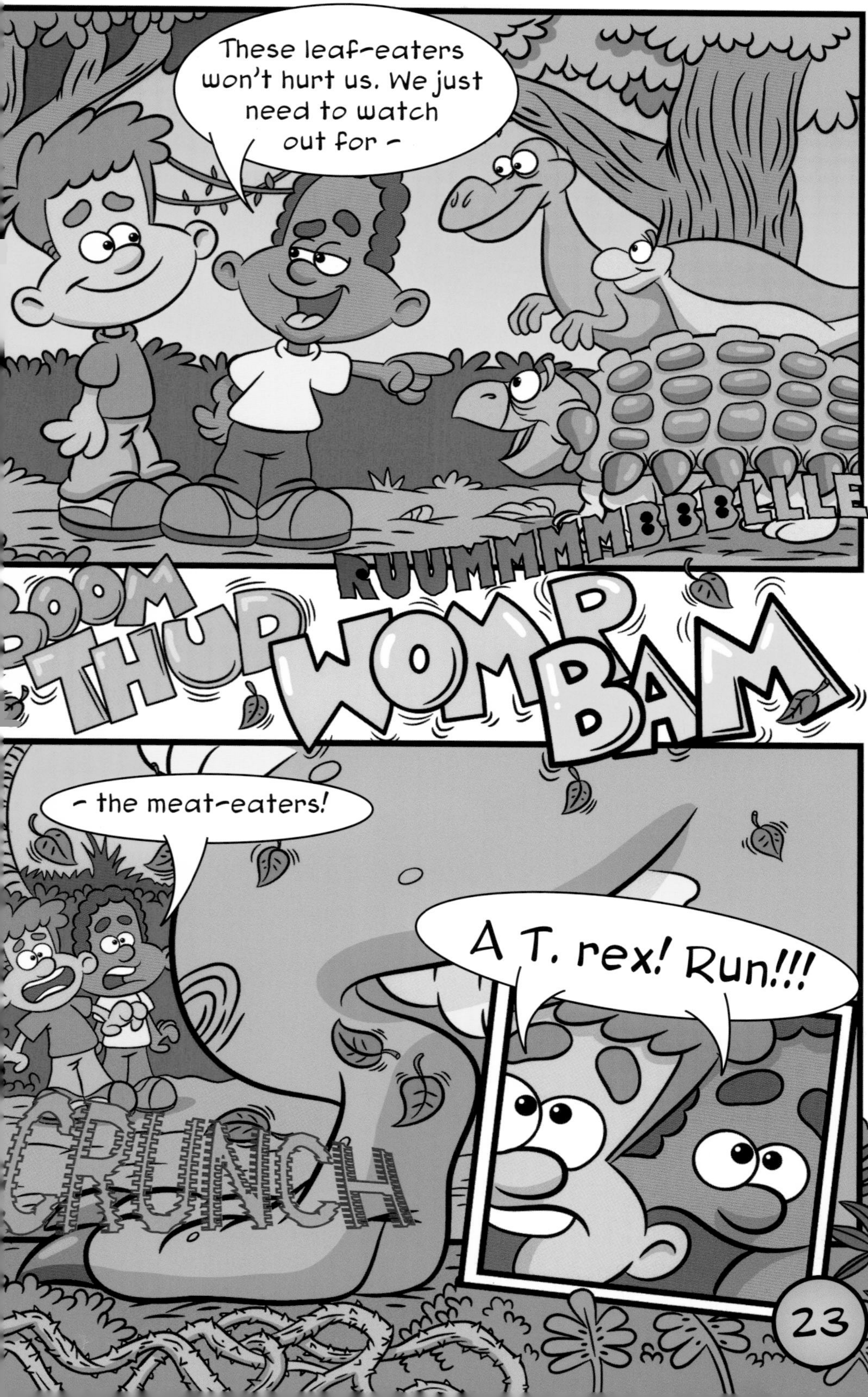
These leaf-eaters won't hurt us. We just need to watch out for -
RUUMMMMMBBBBLLLE
BOOM
THUD
WOMP
BAM
- the meat-eaters!
A T. rex! Run!!!
CRUNCH

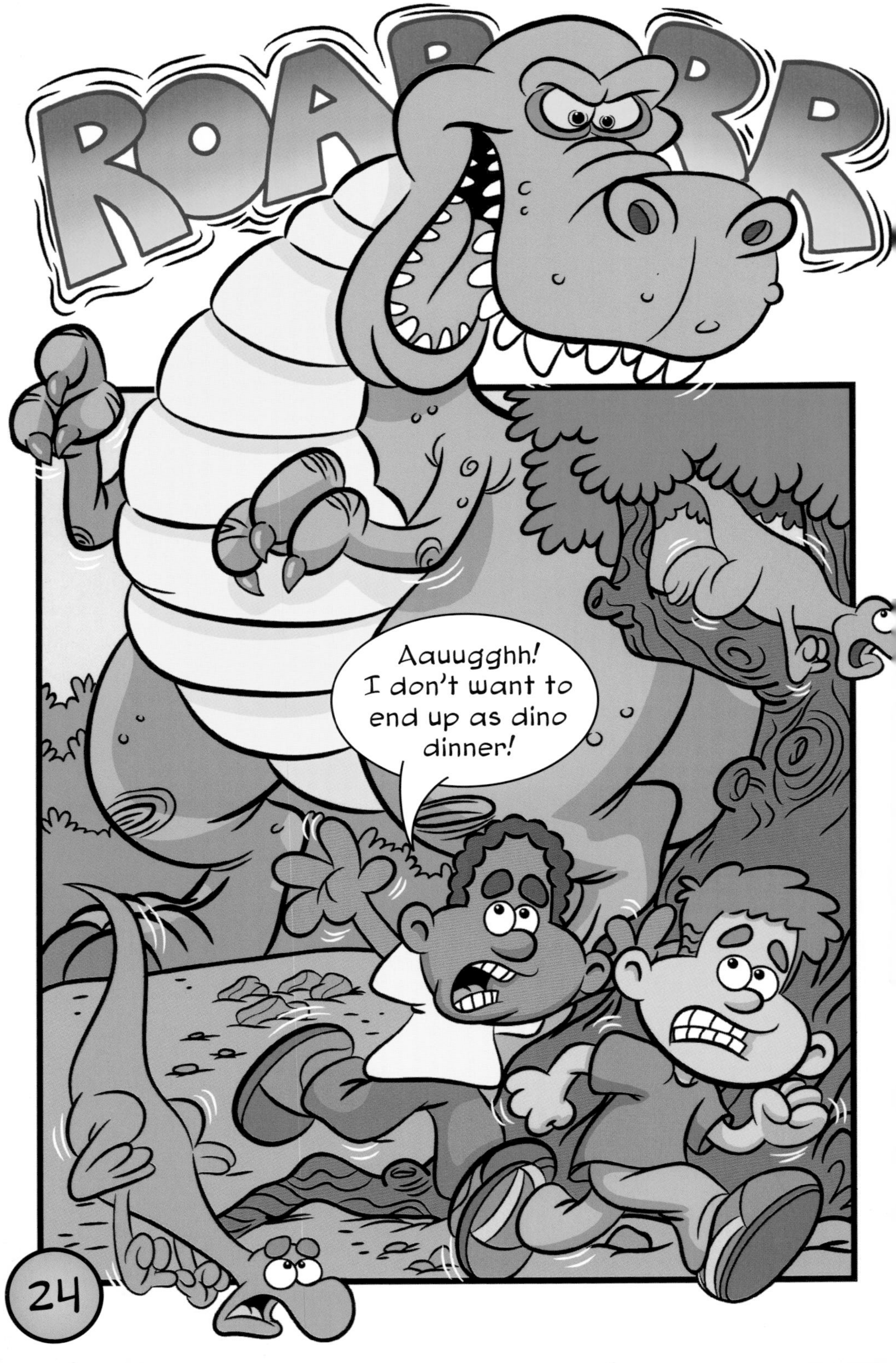
ROARRR
Aauugghh! I don't want to end up as dino dinner!

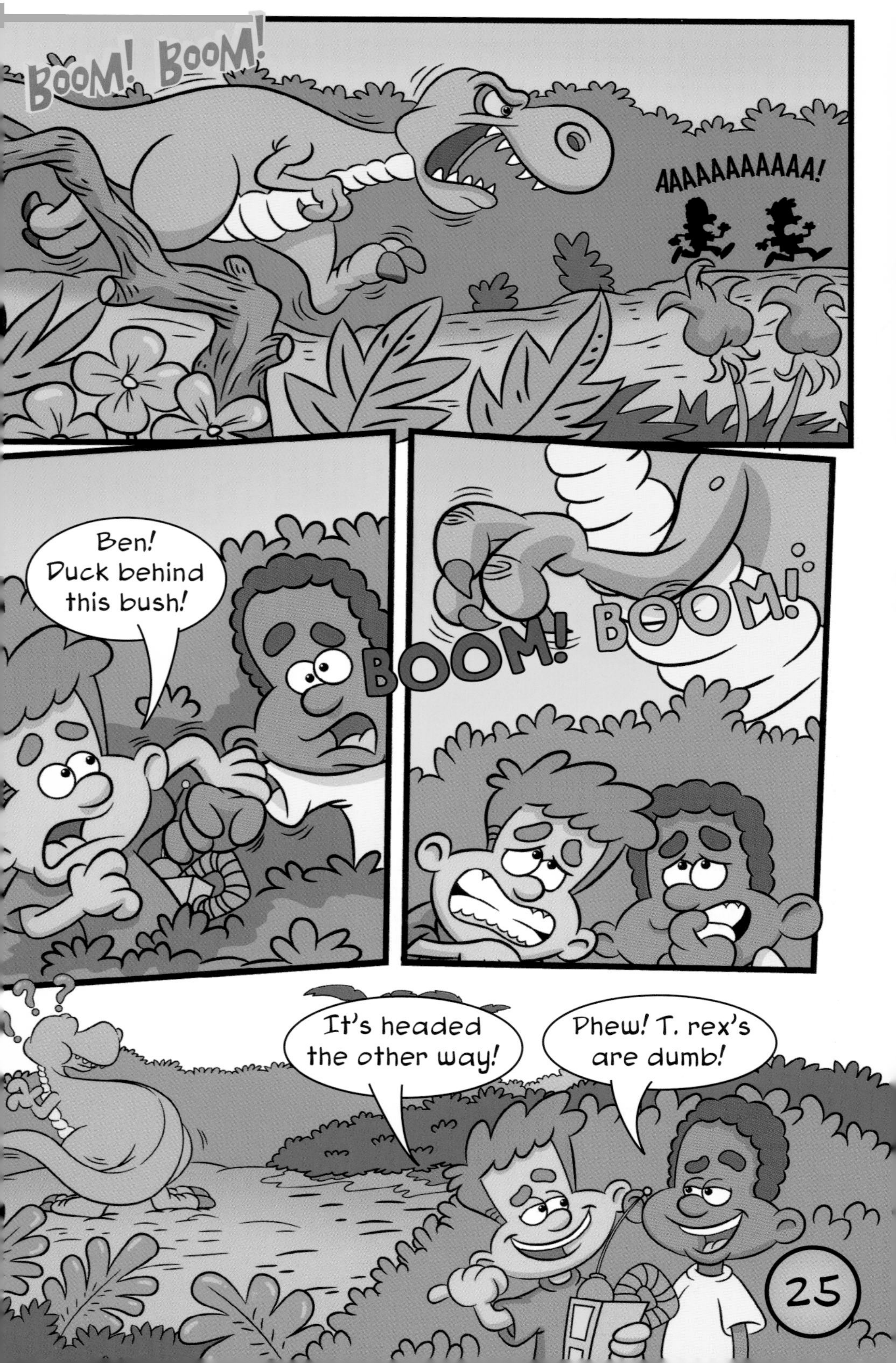

BOOM! BOOM!
AAAAAAAAAAA!
Ben! Duck behind this bush!
BOOM! BOOM! BOOM!
It's headed the other way!
Phew! T. rex's are dumb!

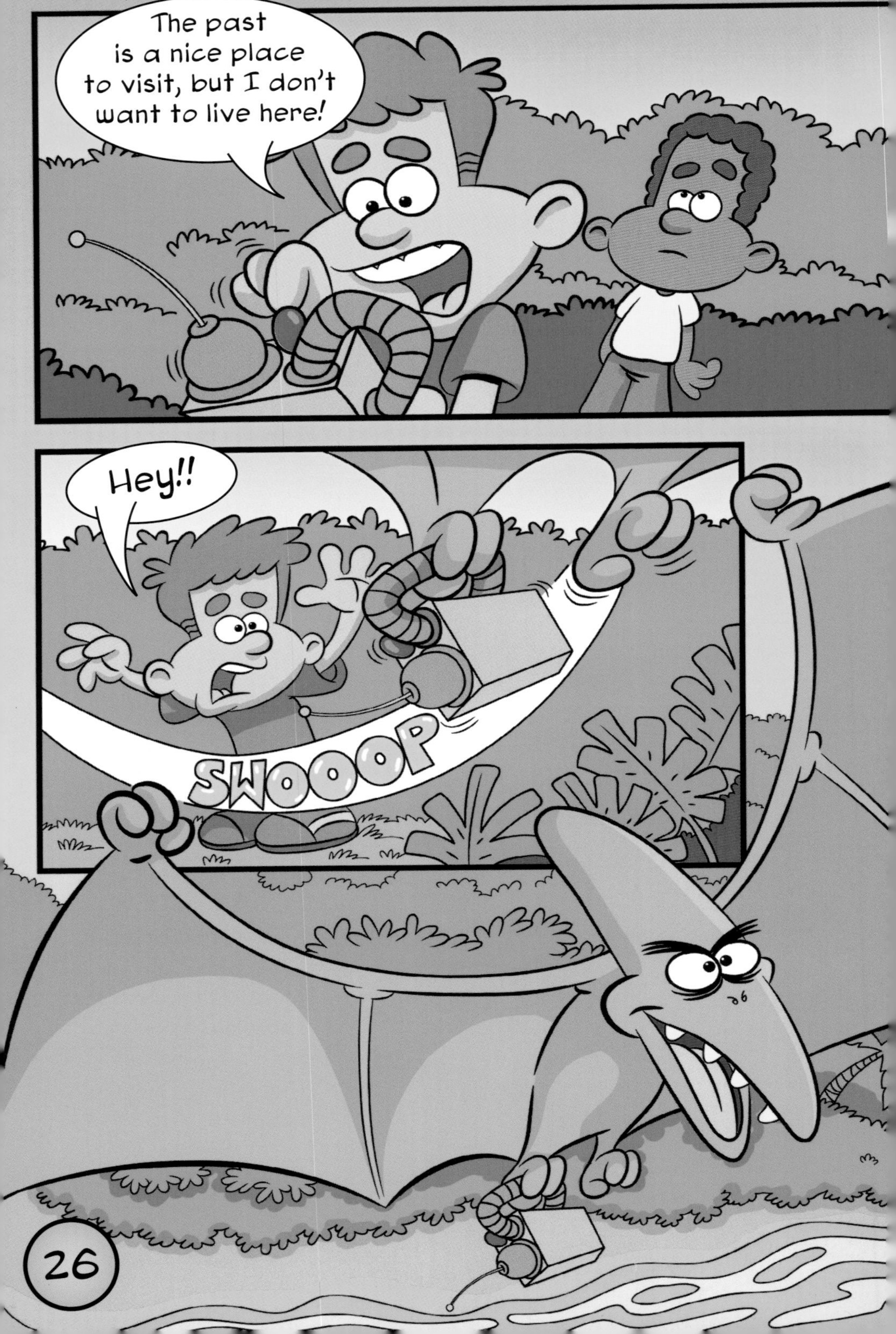
The past is a nice place to visit, but I don't want to live here!
Hey!!
SWOOOP

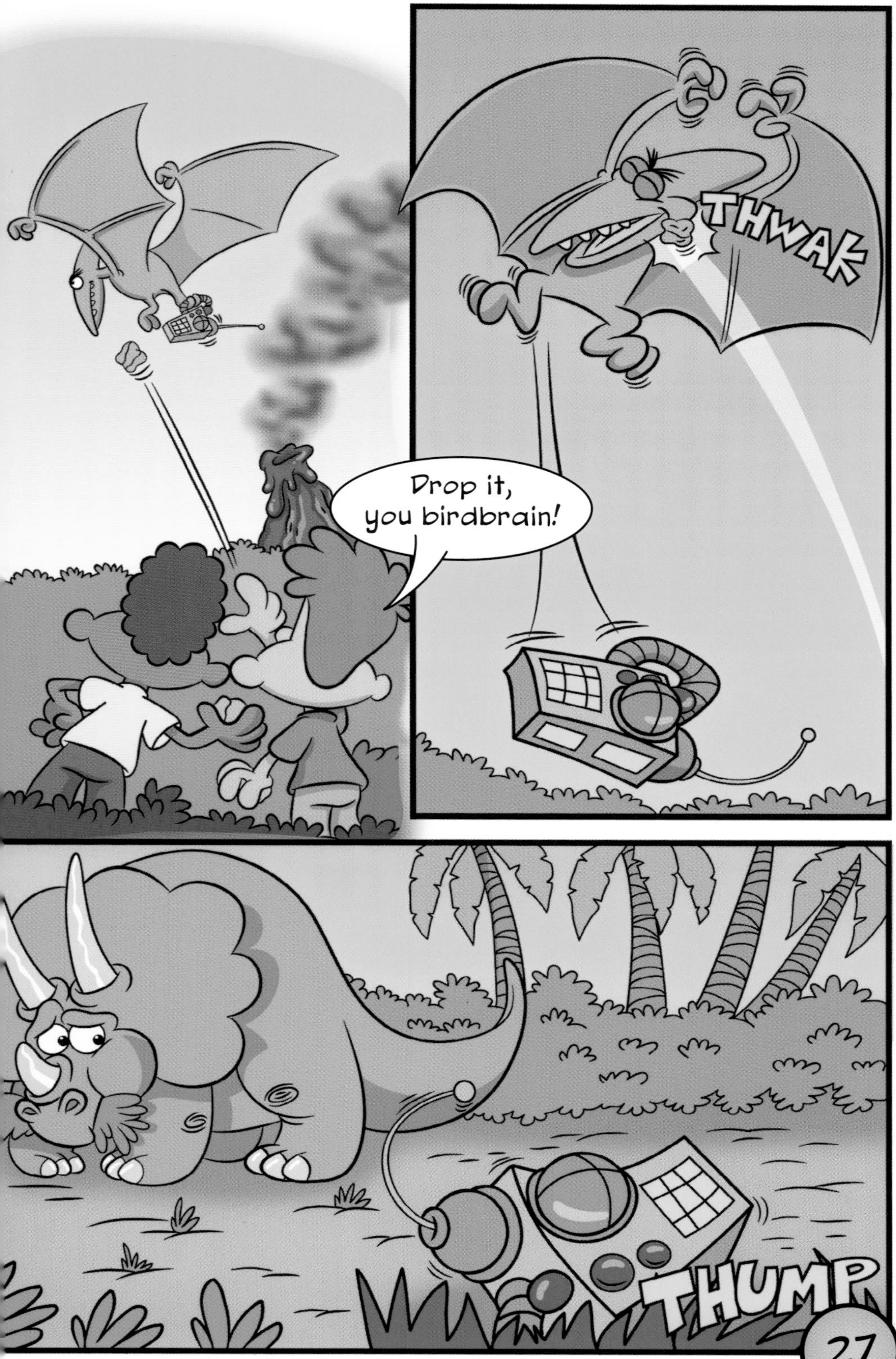
Drop it, you birdbrain!
THWAK
THUMP

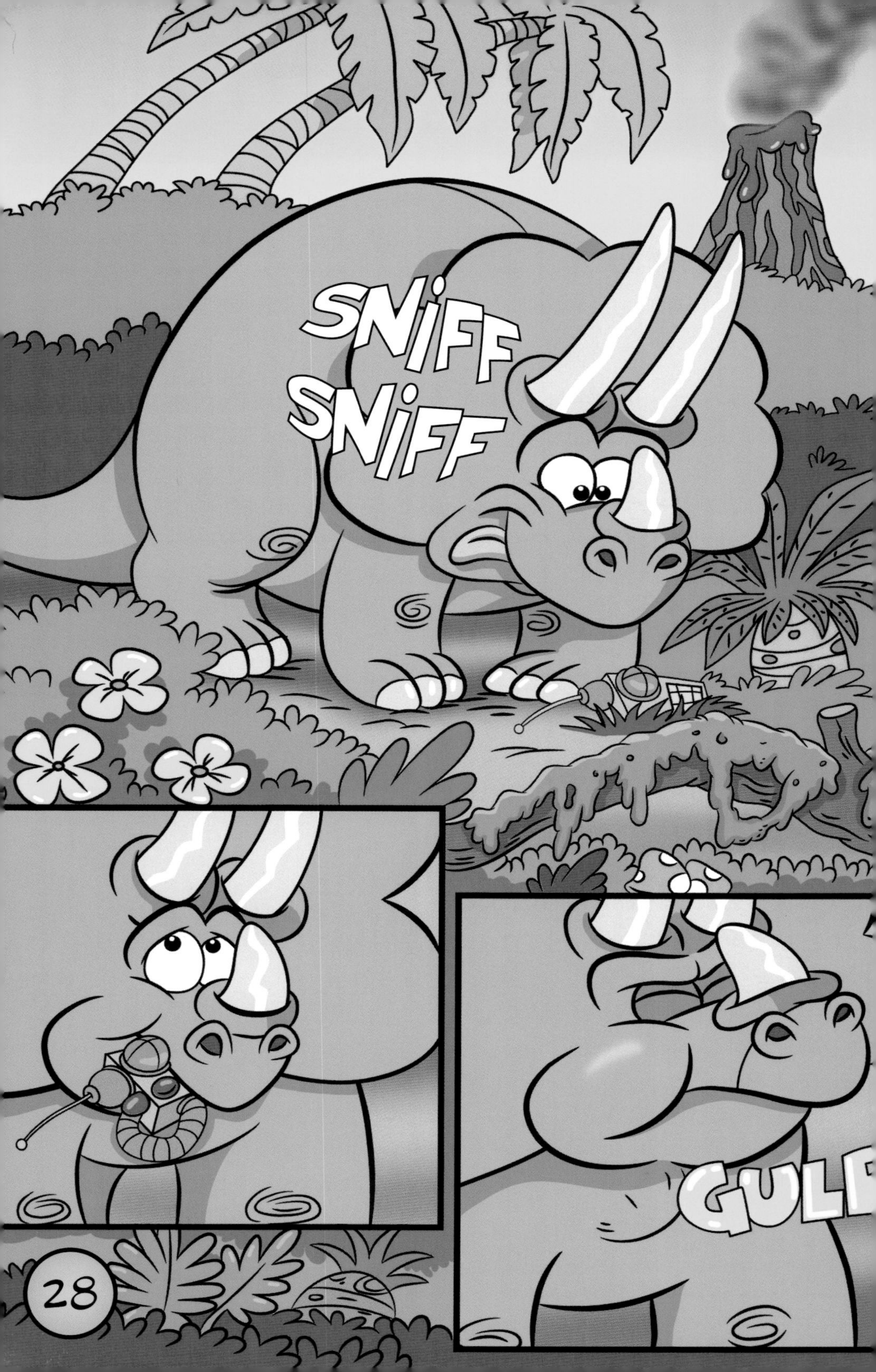
SNIFF
SNIFF
GULP

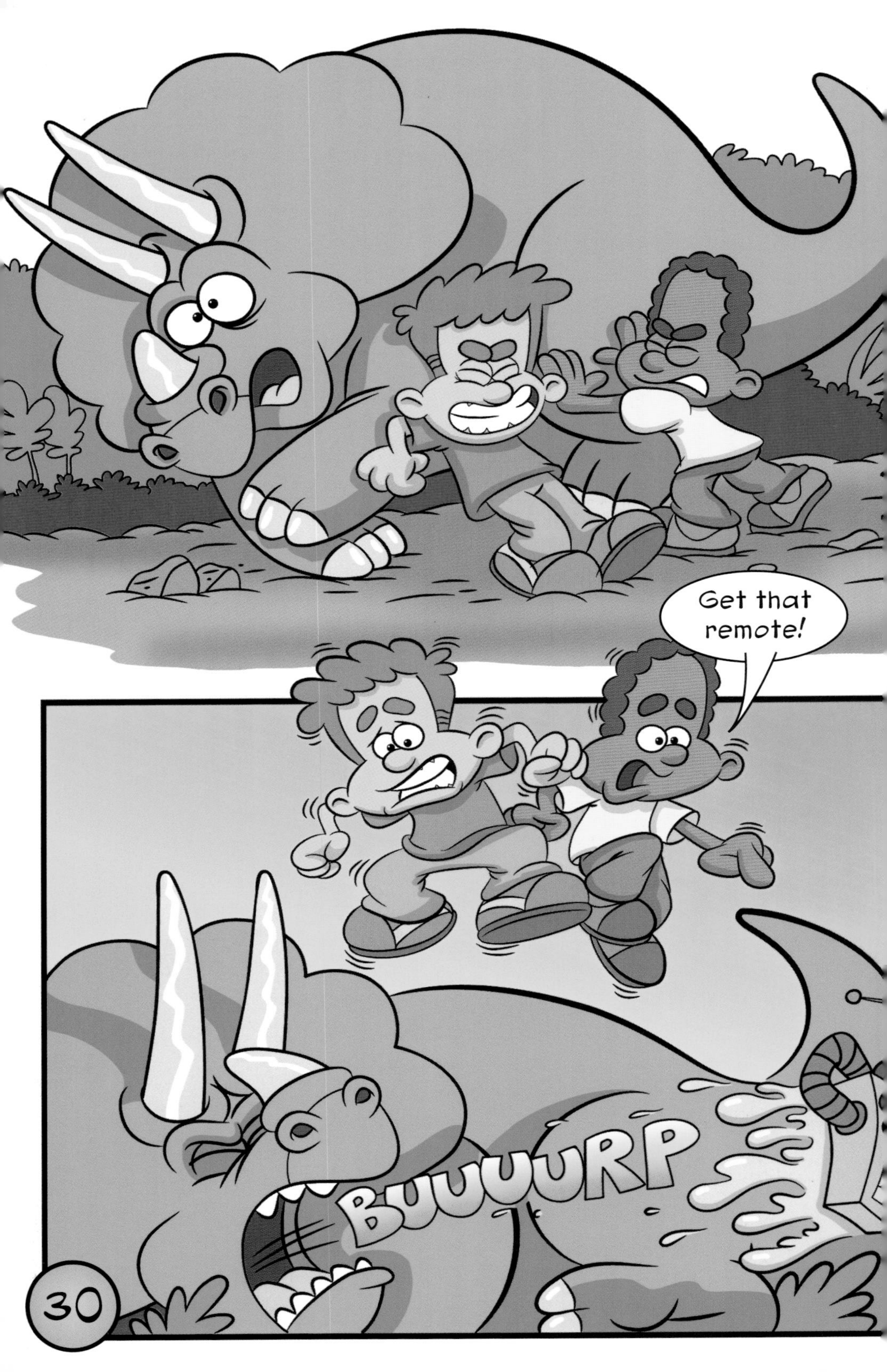
Get that remote!
BUUUURP

31

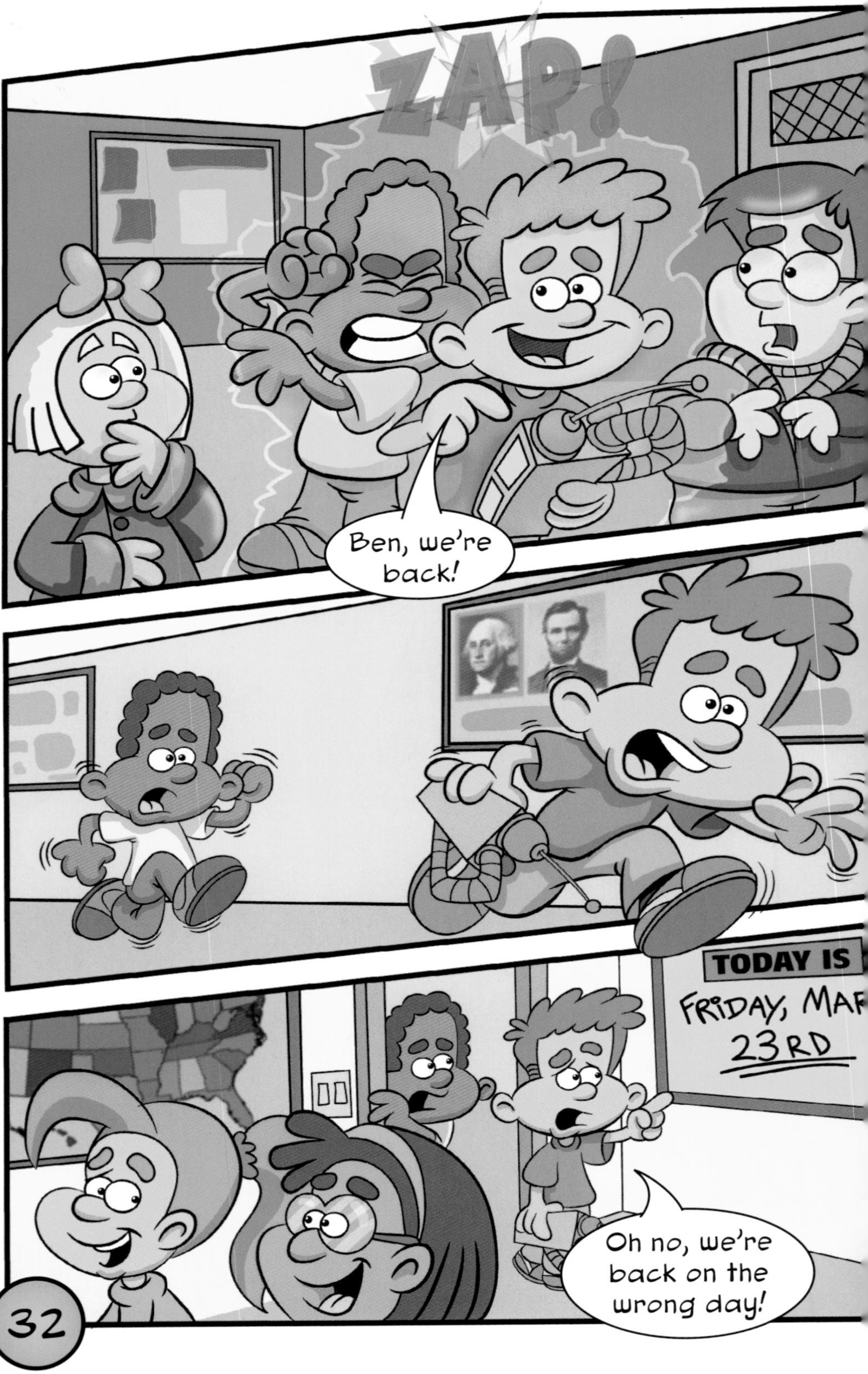
ZAP!
Ben, we're back!
TODAY IS
FRIDAY, MAR
23RD
Oh no, we're back on the wrong day!

ABOUT THE AUTHOR

Scott Nickel has written children's books, short fiction for *Boys' Life Magazine*, humorous greeting cards, and lots of really funny knock-knock jokes. Scott is also the author of many Garfield books.

Currently, Scott lives in Indiana with his wife, two sons, four cats, a parakeet, and several sea monkeys.

ABOUT THE ILLUSTRATOR

Steve Harpster has loved drawing funny cartoons, mean monsters, and goofy gadgets since he was able to pick up a pencil. In first grade, he was able to avoid his writing assignments by working on the pictures for stories instead.

Steve landed a job drawing funny pictures for books, and that's really what he's best at. Steve lives in Columbus, Ohio, with his wonderful wife, Karen, and their sheepdog, Doodle.

GLOSSARY

brachiosaur (BRAK-ee-uh-sor) a long-necked, plant-eating dinosaur that lived more than 150 million years ago

carnivore (KAR-nuh-vor) a meat-eater, like a T. rex or your dog

dino droppings (DYE-noh DROP-ingz) prehistoric poop, also known to scientists as coprolites (KOP-ruh-lites)

eek (EEK) the proper sound to make when you are frightened by the grade on your history test; "ack" will also work.

geek (GEEK) anyone who knows more about computers and science than you do

Ultra Galactic (UHL-truh guh-LAK-tik) the master, or highest, level on the Space Slime Commandos video game

zillionth (ZIL-yuhnth) a lot! More than a jillion, but not as such as a gazillion.

You will be tested on these words, so read up!

DINO BLASTS

Weird facts about dinosaurs

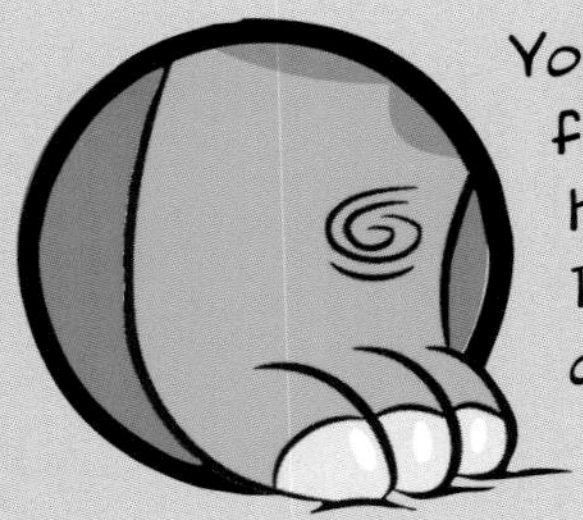

You can tell a plant-eating dinosaur from a meat-eater by noting how many legs they walked on. Plant-eaters usually stomped around on all four legs. Swift and deadly meat-eaters hunted on two legs.

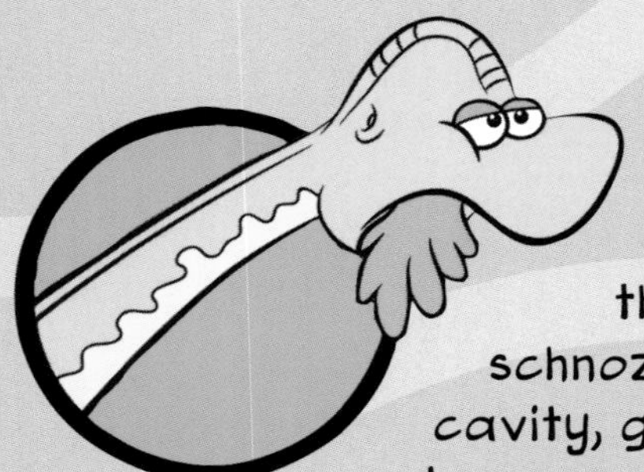

Brachiosaurus had nostrils on the top of its head. Some scientists think the placement of its schnozz, and its large nasal cavity, gave this plant-eater a strong sense of smell.

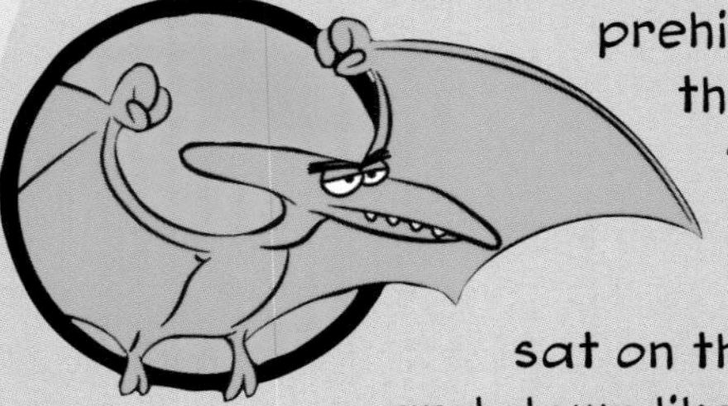

Pteranodon flew over the vast prehistoric oceans, diving into the water to snatch fish. Some scientists think that when this flying creature was tired, it sat on the waves, bobbing up and down like a cork or a duck. A big, **big** duck.

Tyrannosaurus rex had a mouthful of deadly teeth, which were shaped like bananas. But what's with those puny arms? Dino experts think the tiny paws meant that *T. rex* didn't fight for its food but ate creatures that were already dead. Yuck!

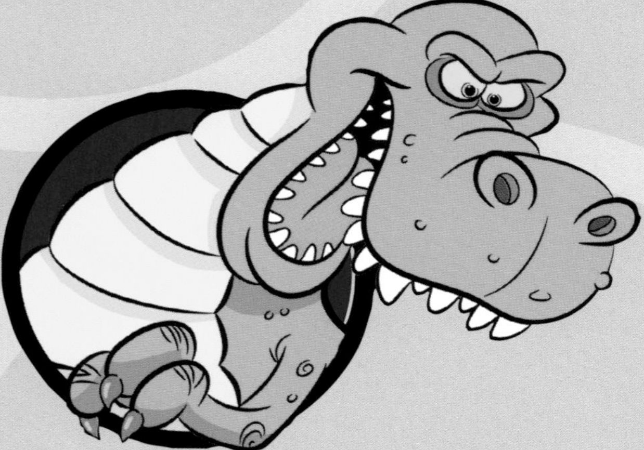

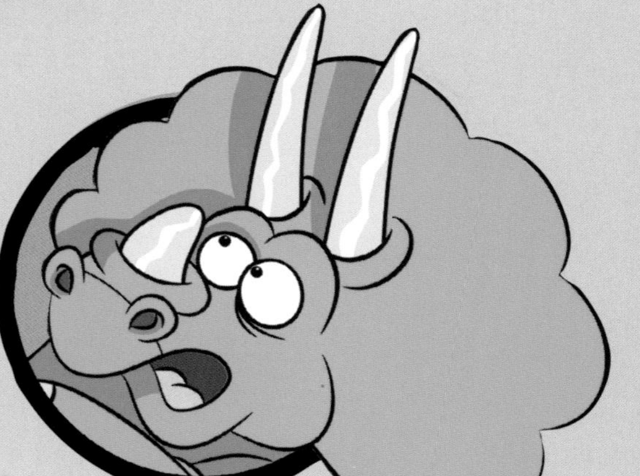

At least one *T. rex* has left its poop behind. Scientists examined the fossilized *doo-doo* and found bone fragments from a *Triceratops*. There's no word on whether this three-horned dino was alive or dead at the time of the meal.

DISCUSSION QUESTIONS

1.) If time machines really existed, would you use one to go back in time to retake a test? Do you think that would be fair?

2.) In books and movies, whenever humans and dinosaurs get together, the dinos attack the puny humans. Do you think this would really happen?

3.) If dinosaurs were available at the local pet store, which one would you want to take home, and why? How do you think your parents or friends would react to your new pet?

WRITING PROMPTS

1.) Everyone makes mistakes. If you could
   go back in time to visit one of your past
   mistakes, which mistake would you choose?
   Write about how you would fix it.

2.) David's geeky brother, Darrin, celebrated
   the invention of his time pod by making a
   giant egg-salad sandwich. If you were
   famous for creating an invention, write
   about what it would be. How would
   you celebrate?

3.) At a nearby mall, a time pod will be set up
   for willing customers. You can travel back to
   prehistoric time and see dinosaurs up close
   and personal. You can take three items along
   on your trip, but only three. Write about
   which ones you would take and why.

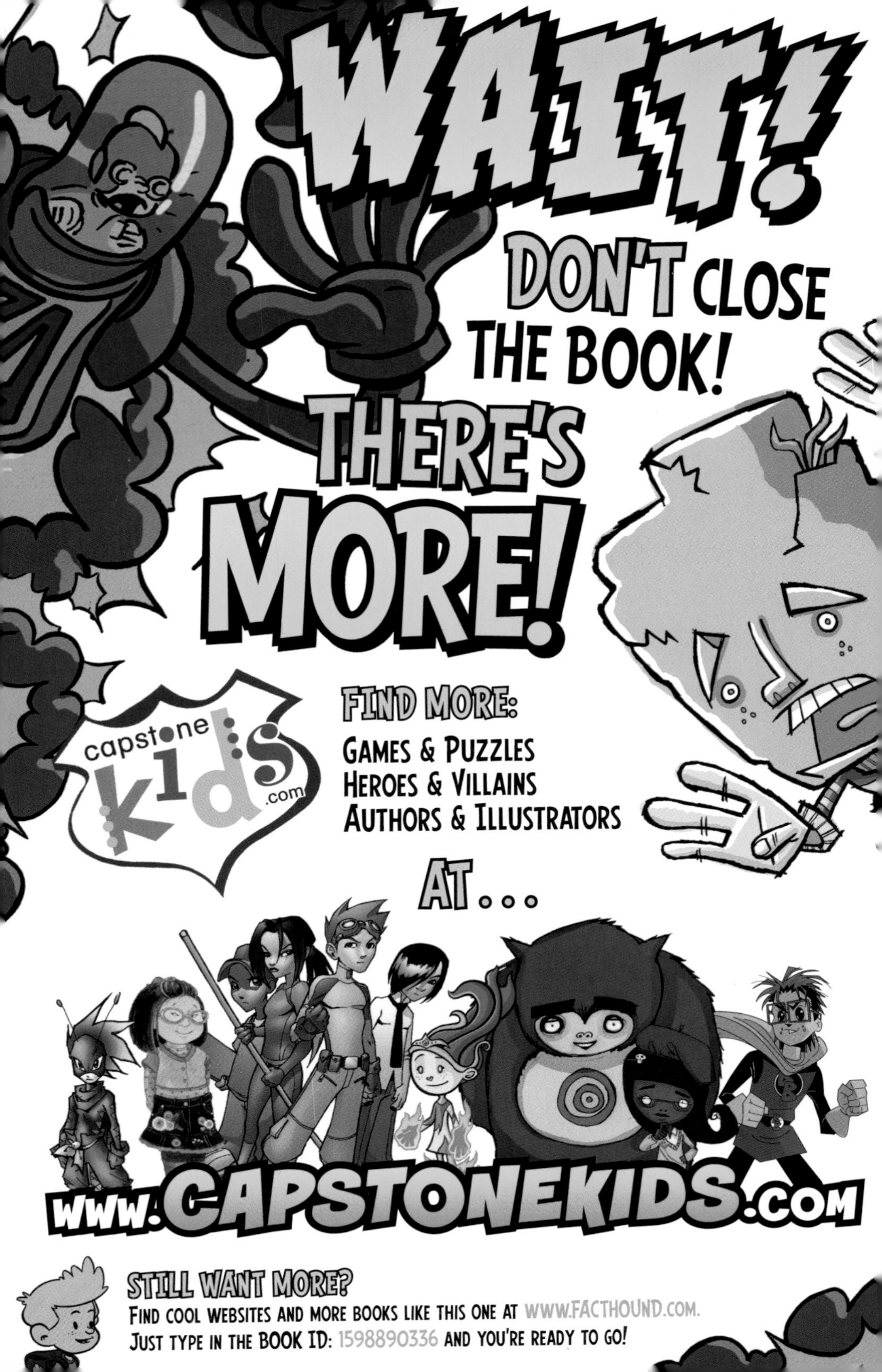
WAIT!
DON'T CLOSE THE BOOK!
THERE'S MORE!
FIND MORE:
GAMES & PUZZLES
HEROES & VILLAINS
AUTHORS & ILLUSTRATORS
AT...
capstone kids .com
WWW.CAPSTONEKIDS.COM
STILL WANT MORE?
FIND COOL WEBSITES AND MORE BOOKS LIKE THIS ONE AT WWW.FACTHOUND.COM.
JUST TYPE IN THE BOOK ID: 1598890336 AND YOU'RE READY TO GO!